An Imprint of Sterling Publishing
387 Park Avenue South
New York, NY 10016

ISBN 978-1-4351-3863-6

Manufactured in Singapore
Lot#:
2 4 6 8 10 9 7 5 3
01/13

Sam Walshaw

Lulu Ladybug

Sandy Creek
NEW YORK

Mrs. Ladybug was having a bad day!

It was washing day, and she
had so much to do.

The baby ladybugs needed feeding, clothes needed mending and the beds needed making too!

"Don't worry Mommy,"
said little Lulu.
"Now I'm a big ladybug,
I can help. I'll go and get all
the things you need – then
you will have less to do!"

"Oh, that would be so helpful, Lulu,"
said Mrs. Ladybug.
So off Lulu flew.

The first person
she met was
Miss Spider.
"Hmm, you look tasty!"
cooed Miss Spider.

"Please don't eat me," cried Lulu.
"I need some thread. If you can spare me some
of yours, you can..." and she whispered
in Miss Spider's ear.
"That would be nice," agreed Miss Spider.

When she got to the pond,
she met Mr. Frog.
"Mmm, you look tasty!"
croaked Mr. Frog,
licking his lips.

"Please don't eat me," said Lulu.
"I need some water, and if you give me
some of yours, you can…" and
she whispered in Mr. Frog's ear.
"Yes please," nodded Mr. Frog.

Lulu bumped into Kitten
playing in the garden.
"Ooh, you look tasty!"
purred Kitten.

"Please don't eat me," squeaked Lulu.
"I need some toys, and if you can give me
one of yours, you can...."
and she whispered in Kitten's ear.
"Lovely!" meowed Kitten.

Then Lulu met Early Bird,
who was looking for worms.
"You look tasty!"
twittered Early Bird.

"Please don't eat me," begged Lulu.
"I need some soft feathers, and if you can
let me have some of yours, you can..."
and she whispered in Early Bird's ear.
"You're on!" trilled Early Bird.
"Phew!" breathed the worm.

Lulu met Mr. Squirrel, who
was collecting nuts.
"You look tasty!"
chattered Mr. Squirrel.

"Please don't eat me!" said Lulu.
"I need some nuts, and if you can give
me some of yours, you can..."
and she whispered in Mr. Squirrel's ear.
"Perfect!" cheered Mr. Squirrel.

Pleased with her
day's work,
Lulu fluttered home.

Her tired Mom was pleased to see her back,
safe and sound.

"Well done, Lulu!"
said Mrs. Ladybug.
"You have saved me so much work.
What a caring little ladybug you are!"

"No problem!" said Lulu. "Everyone was kind and generous. I just had to promise one tiny little thing...

...I promised they could all
come for a party!"

"How nice," sighed a tired Mrs. Ladybug. "You really are a caring little Lulu Ladybug!"

"Goodbye!"